For Catherine
if she wants it

First published 1999
1 3 5 7 9 10 8 6 4 2
Joanna Walsh © 1999
Joanna Walsh has asserted her right under the Copyright Design and Patents Act, 1988
to be identified as the author of this work. First published in the United Kingdom 1999
by Jonathan Cape, Random House, 20 Vauxhall Bridge Road, London SW1V 2SA
Random House UK Limited Reg. No. 954009.
A CIP catalogue record for this book is available from the British Library
ISBN 0 2240 4752 3
Printed in Hong Kong by Midas Printing Ltd

What if?

Joanna Walsh

A Tom Maschler Book
JONATHAN CAPE
London

What if when we got up

Mum and Dad weren't there

and our cat cooked us breakfast?

PRINTED MATTER

LIVRE

宅引越

N° 10

What if, on our way to

BOOK

school, we met a dragon

and had a battle

and took him to school on a string?

What if, when we got to school...

Then I could be a circus girl

I could be a tight rope walker

What if, on our way home,

we were chased by aliens?

My teacher says I shouldn't make things up

My mother says it's all nonsense

But I

say you never know what's round the corner

BOO!